Edited by Veneficia Publications
&
Fi Woods

Typesetting © Veneficia Publications
UK
VENEFICIA PUBLICATIONS UK
veneficiapublications.com

Front cover created using public
domain images modified by
Diane Narraway.
Back cover image courtesy of
Fi Woods LRPS
Additional images are public domain.

Twisted Spell

by

Diane Narraway

Contents

When you come
A knock, knock, knockin'
at Mary's door.
Be very certain,
an' be very sure,
That your intentions are good
an' thy 'eart is pure.
For a knock, knock knocking
On the door of a wytch,
Can see you burn,
an' see you twitch.
Heed the tale
that's far from merry,
An' heed the curse
of Minister Derry.

Chapter 1

Born on the Cusp

Spare the mother,
An' leave the chile
An' watch 'er heart
Grow bitter an' vile.
Leave the mother,
An' spare the chile
An' it will grow
Wicked an' wild.

Mary Flann came into this world shortly after midnight as the last bell rang in the new millennium.

Some say she had no proper birthday—"What with 'er being born on the cusp an' all." Not a child of the old year and not one of the new either. Among the Methodist gossips and naysayers this meant that God had forsaken her. Of course, the fact that her mother had died bringing her into the world didn't go well for Mary or her grandmother, who was left to bring up a young baby in her twilight years. Strictly speaking, Mary's birthday was New Year's Day 1800, and her grandmother Irene was happy to remind folk of this fact at any given opportunity. Olivia Flann, Mary's mother, had several lovers, some of whom were married. Some say she was trying for a bastard, while others just turned the other way when they saw her coming. Wives watched their menfolk, keeping their eyes fixed on them, almost daring them to look when she passed them by. Like her mother, and her grandmother before her, Olivia kept her own counsel, and none would ever know who her child's father was.

The first screams of her labour could be heard late on New Year's Eve. It is said she screamed so loud that it could be heard throughout Chiswell, and even as far as Castletown. It was as if the devil himself was giving birth. So bad was her screaming that her cousin, against his mother's wishes, paid for the doctor to attend. Sadly however, the baby could not be delivered and as the mother grew weaker and the screams fainter, Irene Flann made the heart-breaking decision to save her granddaughter and let her daughter go.

Mary's birth set the tongues wagging; if it wasn't the sound of her mother screaming, it was her lack of father and decent parenting, and so on. Some say she was born of the devil, others claimed that she was herself a devil. Her grandmother was no stranger to gossip, after all, her granddaughter Mary wasn't the first member of the Flann household to set tongues wagging and was unlikely to be the last.

Irene's own mother, allegedly a widow, had brought up Irene and her sister at a time when single mothers were rare. Of course, people didn't really gossip about widows, unless the widow in question was twice widowed.

Irene and Lilian had different fathers, both of whom had died. Given the lack of medical knowledge, poor hygiene, poverty, and often unsanitary conditions, this was not so unusual. Biddy Flann was neither bereft of medical knowledge, nor was she particularly poor or unsanitary, which roused some suspicion. However, given the fact that they both died shortly after their children were conceived, and that they both died suddenly, with no symptoms prior to their deaths made it all seem a lot more dubious.

Initially, when Irene's father Thomas died, the locals assumed it was his fondness for the drink that took him. Irene's mother Biddy, it seemed, had come to the same conclusion, or at least in public she had. However, when Biddy's second husband, Lilian's father, met with the same fate, people weren't so willing to look beyond the widow for the cause of death. Her second husband was a god-fearing man who was popular with the local congregation. The gossip escalated over the following months and eventually, and inevitably, a charge was brought against Biddy Flann: wytchcraft.

As the older sibling by two years, Irene was seven years old when her mother was arrested for wytchcraft in the Autumn of 1775. She remembered all too well the angry mob that burst into their home that warm summer morning. Lily had spent that morning sat in the corner playing with a rag doll Biddy had made a few days previous, when the goodly parishioners of Chiswell burst in filled with righteous fervour. Biddy cautiously steered Irene behind her, towards Lily. The young

Irene watched from the corner, shielding her younger sister as best she could. Although they paid no heed to Biddy's infants, Irene's memories of that day were vivid. She would forever remember her mother being dragged out of the house accompanied by the angry cries of "Wytch! Wytch! She is a Wytch!"

She hadn't put up a fight, but they dragged her, nonetheless. It was brutal, and something Irene would never forget. As frightened as she was, her focus remained on her mother who, she noticed, had grabbed a ginger root from by the door on the way out. Biddy was quite accomplished at growing some of the more exotic roots for healing and, of course, for that which she was being accused of.

As soon as the mob had left with Biddy, the young Irene reached into the jar of freshly cut ginger and grabbed an adequately sized root. Lily, on the contrary, had done nothing other than hide in the corner, sobbing.

'Shh Lily, she'll be fine. Hush yer sobbing, we don't need 'em comin' back just yet.' She dried her little sister's eyes with one hand while twisting the ginger root in the other. Her focus was mainly on the root and the desire to free her mother, while simultaneously attempting to pacify her younger sister.

Both sisters remained huddled in the corner of the kitchen; Irene hugging her sister with her free arm, while her mind stayed fixed firmly on the root in the other hand. She never wavered, not even when the local chaplain, Mr Brackenbury, looked in on them. He was the only man who ever had a kind word to say to the girls, and on this particular morning he had poked his head around the door to check they were alright. He feared they may have been injured during the unruly and unceremonious arrest of their mother.

'I've brought you some of Mrs Brackenbury's gingerbread; she made a fresh batch yesterday.' He crouched down and handed a piece to each of the girls, drying Lily's face with his "handkerchief," as he called it. It was far from the exquisitely decorate handkerchiefs some of the others carried, and closer to a piece of old calico, but it was clean and dry and that was the main thing.

'Thank you,' ventured Irene, 'it's right kind of you Sir.'

'You're welcome,' he smiled, and Lily managed a weak smile back at him.

'That's better' he beamed back at her. 'Now you girls make sure you stay put, and hopefully Biddy will be home soon, and this nonsense will be over and done with.'

'We will an' thank you min'ster.' Irene liked him well enough and was grateful for the gingerbread; Mrs Brackenbury was known for her baking, and it did taste lovely, but Irene had more pressing matters to attend to.

As soon as he had he closed the door behind him, she returned her focus to helping her mother. Fortunately, Lily was quiet now, so it was easier for her to concentrate.

They were alone for what seemed like forever; Lily, pacified by gingerbread and kind words, soon fell asleep. However, Irene's concentration remained solely fixed on the root she had continuously been twisting and turning since her mother's arrest, all the while visualising her mother in the courtroom being found not guilty. And that is how they stayed, with Irene only returning the root to its jar when Biddy Flann returned home a free woman.

'Could feel you in that courthouse,' Biddy remarked, once safely back home. 'Tis a rare gift you have there, girl. I think p'rhaps it's time I taught you all I know.'

Up until then, Irene Flann's life had only really been shaped by her father's death, Lily's birth, and Lily's father who, prior to his death, had been kind enough to her. All of which had led up to that day when her mother returned home a free woman.

She learned her mother's trade fast and Irene Flann grew to be an even more successful herbalist and accomplished cunning woman than Biddy. In her youth it was said that "she had a rare gift" and it did not go unnoticed that she, Irene Flann, was a "pretty lass" and by all accounts had her fair share of suitors.

Lily, on the contrary, wanted no part of it; she heard how they gossiped about her mother and sister. It was the fear she remembered from her mother's arrest, more than the actual event and as much as she loved them both, they could carry on without her.

She sought work in the Brackenbury house as a maid, and Minister Brackenbury treated her as well as any man could treat a servant. She had a good life, and shortly after her 16th birthday she met a young quarryman, Samuel Peters. He was a good Christian, who earned an honest wage. Lily was a beauty, probably more so than Irene, but Irene had a different way about her, something that made her stand out.

The moment Lily caught Samuel Peters' attention, he was besotted by her; she was quiet, kind, beautiful, and above all, nothing like her family. They were soon married, and Lily went on to have five children, the youngest of which was William Peters.

Irene never married, but did have a child, and her bastard daughter, Olivia, looked just a little too much like Lily's son William.

Irene was brazen, and while she was never accused of wytchcraft, people gossiped about her sexual exploits, and William was all of Lily's worst fears come true. He was just like

Irene, and Lily feared that Olivia might have been William's half-sister and not his cousin.

The truth of the matter was that Lily and Irene were actual sisters, not half-sisters, with neither of them having been conceived by their alleged fathers. Despite all the whispers and rumours, Biddy had taken their father's identity to her grave and Irene looked set to do the same. For Lily, there was no escaping the fact that William's dark eyes and, worse still, his behaviour was a whole lot more like Irene's than hers.

Biddy passed away early in 1778, and while her funeral had been sparsely attended, the most notable absence was her youngest daughter Lily. Irene, of course, had taken over the family business and had to work twice as hard as she may otherwise have had to in order to undo her family's bad name. An accusation of wytchcraft can damage the name of any family. Apart from her mother's funeral, Irene, like Biddy, never set foot in any of the island's churches.

Some things are just in the blood.

Olivia Flann, of course, would go on to be a healer and a cunning woman, while her cousin, William Peters, concerned himself with local government. Despite their similarities and Lily's concerns, their paths were vastly different, but William was a good ally to the Flann women.

Olivia would also become the mother of a baby girl, and like all Flann cunning women, she too was born out of wedlock. A bastard girl born on the cusp of the millennium named Mary Flann.

Chapter 2
The Wytch of Chiswell

Mix fresh skullcap,
An' crampbark,
With a dash of mugwort,
For she's the mother of all 'erbs.
Mix 'em well
An' mix 'em true,
To ease the plight of birth.

Bridie Peters was born a few hours after Mary Flann, in what was a far less dramatic event. In fact, there were three baby girls born that night, and none with as much fuss as the Flann girl. Bridie's mother did survive. Her husband William's mother Lily, having swallowed her pride, had bought some herbs from her sister Irene Flann.

Every footstep she took towards that accursed apothecary, she felt was a step closer to hell. It was only a short walk from her home to Biddy's Apothecary, as Irene had named it after their mother's death.

'In 'onour of our mother.' Irene had announced, as Lily had eyed up the sign in the window.

12

'In 'onour of a wytch.' Lily had corrected her, spitting the words, before adding, 'Shame on you Irene, folk round 'ere 'as long mem'ries. You are no better than she was.' This was followed by her sticking her nose in the air and walking away, but not without one final huff.

That was twelve years ago, at a time when she was still wracked with rage towards her sister, believing that Olivia had been the bastard child of her beloved Samuel. Of course, she had never voiced this, but she knew plenty had.

Did they not think she could hear them, or see their pitiful looks? Of course she could, and every single one fuelled her bitterness.

In that way that the world has of fulfilling the prophecies of the self, eventually Samuel found his way to Irene's bedchamber. Lily was right about her sister's brazen lack of moral compass where matters of the flesh were concerned. Samuel died a few short years later of the pox.

Everyone knew it but no one dared mention it. But as before, Lily knew they all thought it.

13

However, now being forced to enter that cursed apothecary was more than she could bear. She must have stood across the street staring at it for a fair time, as she caught the attention of Irene's bastard offspring, the heavily pregnant Olivia.

'Hey, Auntie Lily,' she shouted, heading towards her.

—*Dear Lord,* she thought.

—*The child is as brazen as 'er mother.*

'Hello Olivia. I need this,' the words came out so quickly they almost tripped over themselves as she thrust the list into her niece's hand.

'I'll get 'em sorted out for you and drop 'em round later.' Lily didn't venture a response, she just turned and hurried off up the road, hoping that her mortal soul was still intact.

It was Irene who dropped the small package to Lily later that day; she had hoped to talk, but Lily had no intention of speaking to her harlot sister.

'You know Lily …'

'Yes, I know only too well. Thank you for the 'erbs an' good day.'

She was quite proud of herself for standing up to the "Wytch of Chiswell," as she constantly referred to her. She wished, but only ever silently and always followed by a prayer of forgiveness, that Irene had also died of the pox. And the fact that her husband had died of it, while Irene remained the picture of health was just further proof that her sister was a wytch. Plain and simple.

Lily, bitter and twisted as she was, vowed to outlive her sibling.

When the news spread that Olivia had gone into labour, Lily hoped neither her nor her child would survive. Perhaps if they died, then Biddy's cursed bloodline would end. Obviously, she, having distanced herself many years ago, no longer considered herself as being part of that lineage.

So, when the screams rang out throughout Chiswell, seeing the old year out and the new year in. Lily raised a glass outwardly toasting to better days and peace in our time, and inwardly toasting the end of Irene's family. The following morning Lily was mortified to hear the child had survived.

'Born on the cusp she was. Mrs Peters an' my ma says near on ripped her clean in two it did ... an' bein' born on the cusp too ... well, you know what that means?' Jimmy White tapped his nose knowingly. Lily just nodded gravely, of course she knew what it meant. Another bastard Flann wytch had entered the world. She doubted, however, that young Jimmy White, the grocer's boy, had the vaguest idea what it meant and neither did she care much.

The important thing was that William's bastard half-sister was dead but, unfortunately, had delivered another healthy and, no doubt, brazen wytch into their god-fearing community.

William's wife went into labour shortly after and delivered a beautiful healthy girl, who William named Bridie.

'Isn't she a beauty, Ma?' He proudly announced, beaming from ear to ear. 'Reckon she'll 'ave 'er pick of the lads.'

'Don't talk like that William. She's only a babe.'

'Oh, for the love of God, Mother; stop. The Flann women 'ave done nothing bad to us, an' wasn't it their 'erbs what 'elped bring this beauty into the world? Enough is enough!'

Lily left the room before she said something she'd regret. Such was her bitterness, and anger towards Irene and her new granddaughter.

The rain fell heavily, almost as heavily as Lily's tears, as the coffin bearing the name of William Peters was lowered into its final resting place. Had it not been enough that she had lost her beloved Samuel? Now it seemed that her son had also been destined to die young. And worse still, had also died of the pox. Clearly, William had the same morals as his father.

Lily was heartbroken and hated Irene Flann, even more now, believing her responsible for all the ills that had befallen her once-happy household. It seemed only a short while ago that she and Samuel had welcomed William into the world, and now here she was bidding him a heartbroken farewell. She cursed the name of Irene Flann.

Chapter 3
A Perfect Name

An ugly girl,
Is a mother's shame,
Though pure of heart.
A mother's sorrow,
An' who's to blame?
Her wicked ways,
Or his darker deeds
Either can cause a poison
In his seed.

Eliza Pearce, or Elsie as she was commonly known, was born a few hours after Mary Flann and Bridie Peters. Her family was not initially from Portland, both her parents having been born in the county town. However, they had moved to the island when their eldest child was only a few months old.

Elizabeth, Elsie's mother, was a determined woman who had set her sights on Joseph "Joe" Pearce when she was around ten years old. She had always intended to marry him, and he had little say in the matter. Elizabeth was not one to take "No" for an answer.

Once married, she settled down to the business of running the household.

She ran her house like a well-kept boarding house and her family likewise. Joe was now Mr Joseph Pearce and to his four children, "Sir." If nothing else, her family would have impeccable manners and her husband would have respect.

Joe Pearce had been working as an assistant gardener, but the pay was too low for a family man. So, when Elizabeth fell pregnant with their first child, at her request, Elizabeth's well-connected father managed to find him work and a house, but it meant moving to Portland. There wasn't any refusing Elizabeth; Joseph had learnt that long ago. And so, they arrived on the island as newlyweds, with a child already on the way, on July 6th, 1778.

Mr Joseph Pearce was now a quarryman and quickly, with Elizabeth by his side, became site manager. This meant they were able to buy a significantly larger house. They may not have been island-born, but Elizabeth made damn sure that despite being Kimberlins[1] they were island-

accepted. They had four children with very little age difference between them and Elizabeth managed her children the same way she managed her husband, at arm's length and with the utmost efficiency.

Joseph was a god-fearing man and like most of the island had joined the Methodist church. He and his wife attended every Sunday without fail. He made very few physical demands on Elizabeth, which suited her fine. As a rule, like most god-fearing men, he visited The Jolly Sailor in Castletown, which was known for its fine ales and equally fine women. This suited Elizabeth provided her husband was discreet, or as discreet one possibly can be in such a small community.

Over the years she, Elizabeth, became grandmother to three children. She was settled and her husband earned a good wage. Life was good.

And then it happened!

Joseph came home from work late one evening in the April of 1799. Elizabeth rightly assumed he had gone from work to the Jolly Sailor.

'Joseph, I need to talk to you.'

She announced sternly.

'Uuuh er'

Elizabeth was in no mood to attempt a serious conversation with a drunken idiot fresh from a whore's bed. She marched straight to the scullery and returned with a full pitcher of water, which she promptly slung in his face.

'Are you out of yer mind woman?' he spluttered angrily, as he squared up to her, soaked, and with water still dripping from his face.

'You lay one hand on me, and I'll scream so loud ... So help me I will. Do you hear me?'

'I 'ear ya.' he said sitting back down. 'I've never raised me 'and to a woman and I'm not about to start now, but I would like to know what's so urgent that I 'ave to be so rudely awoken.'

Elizabeth Pearce placed the empty pitcher on the table and smoothed her skirts demonstratively.

'Well,' she began tentatively, 'I've missed my ... well ... you know?' she urged him quietly.

Joseph Pearce might have been awake but awake doesn't necessarily mean alert or capable of any rational thought. Instead, he looked up at her, towering over him with her arms folded, hoping for a clue.

'My time has passed—or rather, hasn't passed.'

She desperately hoped he would understand, as this was not a subject she was comfortable discussing with anyone. It was hopeless. The blank expression on his face and helpless look in his eye; he hadn't the vaguest idea what she was talking about.

'I have missed my courses.' She had dropped her voice to a whisper, afraid that God himself might hear her and strike her down for her wicked tongue.

Joseph looked none the wiser.

'I am with child ... with child, I tell you. Was that really so difficult to understand?!'

'Yer 'avin' a baby? But 'ow? Ain't you too old?'

'Why Joe Pearce, I ought ...' but she never finished her sentence. She had called him "Joe Pearce." She had dropped all her airs and graces, and in that moment he loved her, and he wanted her, even more than he had wanted her the first time. Within an instant he was up and kissing her for all he was worth, and she, too, wanted him as much, if not more than ever. He picked her up, lifting her onto the dining table so fast she scarcely had time to draw breath. She hitched up her nightdress and he fucked her like he never had before; not aggressively, not desperately, or urgently, but softly, attentively, and lovingly. He knew from that moment on, his whoring days were behind him. Elizabeth, his wife, had given him his youth back and he loved her for it, and from here on in, he would always love her.

Elizabeth watched the ice outside the window form crystalline patterns on the ledge; each one unique and each one beautiful. The fire was rarely left to burn down these days and the room was warm and cosy. Joe, as she now referred to him, would be home soon and she hoped he would remember to fetch the tincture she had asked for from Irene Flann. In the meanwhile, she returned to her chair at the fireside and resumed her embroidery.

It had been a good many years since her and Joe had shared a bed, but she vowed that once her confinement was over and her baby nursed, she would once again take up her marital duties. This time, however, it would be out of love not duty, her desire instead God's law. Throughout her confinement, Joe had been an attentive and loving husband. Some nights he had come to her chamber to read to her, some nights he would take supper with her, and idly chat; at other times he came seeking solace and relief. The act of intercourse was, of course, frowned upon during confinement, but a resourceful wife can oblige her husband in many ways, and oblige him she did, willingly. She looked forward to his nightly visits, whatever they involved, and they grew closer than ever.

On this occasion, Joe returned from work to share supper with his wife and had remembered to collect the tincture from Irene Flann.

'Irene asked after you; she said it can't be long now … is it? Long, I mean?'

'Yes Joe ... or rather no, not long,' she laughed. 'The good Lord knows how many times I've told you I'm due mid-January, but the way things feel I'm sure it will be sooner.'

''Ow much sooner? An' what's the wytch's brew for?'

'Joe Pearce, she'll have your guts for garters if she hears you call her a wytch; she's a skilled lady in many ways, is Irene. You'd think those around'd be grateful for her knowledge. And, in answer to your question, it's for making sure the baby is strong and healthy when it does arrive.'

'So, only another two weeks then?'

Elizabeth nodded. Joe had obviously not read the request when he had taken it to Irene, so was oblivious to the post-script asking for an additional something to quicken the pregnancy. Irene, of course, had obliged and Elizabeth began her labour the following evening.

'Joe ... Joe ... come quickly ... NOW!! Fetch Irene, fetch Irene; the baby's on its way.'

'Bloody 'ell ... You said two weeks' Joe got his coat and hat on, much slower than she would've liked, and headed out into the cold dark street.

'Joe, please hurry.' She called after him, but he couldn't hear her against the icy wind and closing door.

Irene swaddled Mary in several blankets and looked at her daughter, cold and still. The tears welled up in her eyes and she fought to keep them back; it was too cold for either tears or new-born babies. She carried the image of her daughter along with her baby granddaughter as she followed Joe Pearce through the streets.

Despite having lost her only daughter just a few hours ago, Irene wasn't one to leave a soul in distress.

It seemed like an eternity before Joe and Irene returned, but with her arrival things became much easier.

The women of the island preferred to keep things simple, like they always had been. The doctor wasn't called for childbirth—that was the domain of women.

What does a man know of confinement and labour?

She reached Elizabeth's chamber and placed the young Mary in the arms of a bewildered Joe Pearce and ushered him out of the room.

Irene took a deep breath, pushed her grief to the back of her mind, rolled up her sleeves, and got on with the job of delivering Elizabeth Pearce's baby.

Elizabeth was badly in need of a midwife—being an older mother, her age was against her.

'There, there, Elizabeth.' Irene patted Elizabeth's hand reassuringly. She could see the fear in Elizabeth Pearce's eyes. Too many women died in childbirth.

'Don't fret so; you'll be fine, just take deep breaths. Long and slow—long and slow. That's much better, now let's get this littl'un into the world.'

Irene's knowledge of such matters made things a lot easier than they might otherwise have been.

It was a long and arduous labour and left Irene no time to grieve for Olivia. Nor was there time to worry about the young Mary, who managed to sleep throughout the whole event, safe in the arms of Elizabeth's husband.

Eliza Pearce came into the world in the dawn twilight of January 1st,

1800. It was a bitter cold winter morning, and her first cries could be heard just as the snowflakes began to settle on the ground outside.

'She's too little to be an Eliza; I think she should be an Elsie.' were Joe's first words upon seeing the tiny girl, only minutes old.

'I like Eliza; it's a perfectly fine name, and besides, it's the start of Elizabeth ... Isn't that a nice name?' Joe blushed, the last thing he wanted to do was upset his wife. She had, after all, just given birth to his youngest daughter.

"Ow about we call her Eliza, all official like, but she can be our Elsie. Like a pet name ... does that sound agreeable?'

She smiled up at her husband.

'That sounds more than fine Joe, it sounds perfect.

She was the youngest of five children and by far and away the least aesthetically pleasing, but she had melted her father's heart. Her mother, however, knew what folk said and being an avid social climber, she constantly had to remind herself that despite her unfortunate looks, her youngest still deserved to be treated kindly. While her mother may have tried very hard to remind herself of this, the fact remained that, on many occasions, her youngest's appearance was a bit of an embarrassment.

As Elsie grew up she remained the apple of her father's eye and could wrap him around her little finger. Her mother, however, was not so easily won over and despite Elizabeth's obvious disapproval, Elsie became firm friends with Bridie Peters and Mary Flann.

It was a sunny autumn day when Elsie met the other two at the local schoolhouse. It was run by Miss Dunning, who had recently moved to the island. Many viewed her with suspicion, what with her being a Kimberlin. However, she was well educated and forward-thinking and offered an education to those girls whose parents could afford it. Being a 'forward-thinking woman' herself, Irene Flann had used what savings she had amassed to educate her granddaughter. This was a luxury previous Flann women hadn't the opportunity to indulge in, nor need of if truth be told. Bridie Peters' family could easily afford to educate their daughter and as for Elsie, well, Elizabeth made sure she was among the select few. After all, Elsie didn't have much else going for her, so, at the tender age of six, the three girls became classmates, and subsequently friends.

There were some who said the girls were destined to be friends on account of their birthdays, while others viewed them with suspicion. Three well-educated girls were not the norm, and when one was already considered a wytch ... Well, people talk don't they? That said, as far as Elsie Pearce was concerned, she may not have been blessed with looks, but there was none with a kinder heart and that was something no one could dispute. And of course, they were all regular faces in church, even the young Mary Flann.

So, however odd the trio might have been, they were, for the most part, left in peace.

---

1 Kimberlin ... Local slang for any strangers living on, but not native to the Isle of Portland.

Chapter 4
A Simple Act of Kindness

Be wary of
The little chile of God,
Whose soul is pure,
But 'ome hag rod.[1]
When left alone,
With only 'er thoughts,
She'll bury 'er past
With bones and roots.

Martha Wiggot was one of God's own. She had a beautiful soul and a pretty face. Her mother had died when she was young, and she was brought up by her father, who never remarried. He had a smallholding: a few fruit trees and some livestock, mostly sheep and chickens. He sold jams and fleeces down at Chiswell market and always had Martha in tow. There was plenty of gossip as to whether he was lavishing his affections on Martha somewhat inappropriately. This came mostly from the women, as plenty of the menfolk had come across him at the Jolly Sailor. However, they weren't about to admit that to their wives, for fear of reprisal. There are just some things that are best kept quiet. John Wiggot was, like most of the islanders, a devout Methodist and regularly attended church, almost as regularly as he attended the Jolly Sailor. Like most men on Portland at that time, he sinned on Saturday and repented on Sunday. Martha was brought up to be a good "God-fearing" Methodist, who worked hard, studied the bible, and paid no heed to gossip.

Late in the Autumn of 1813, when Martha was only 12, John Wiggot was taken ill with what Irene Flann informed her was consumption. Irene was an authority on consumption as she herself was suffering from it. Martha nursed her father as he spat blood and became weaker and weaker. She mopped up after him and watched as he slowly wasted away, eating less and less of the food she prepared for him. The end was inevitable, and, for all her compassion, she was tired. Trying to nurse a sick father, keep up with the chores around the smallholding, and sell produce at market was taking its toll. She felt tired and older than her years.

It was around Yuletide that Martha made the decision to seek out Mary Flann. Irene had passed back in November and, having watched her grandmother slowly waste away from the disease, Martha felt Mary might be sympathetic to her.

'Well, well. We don't see you down 'ere much these days, but I've no need to guess what brings you to my shop.'

'No Mary. I don't suppose you do.'

''Ow's your father?'

'Not good. Well, truth to tell, 'e can't 'ave long left, and I feel like I've done all I can. So, I was 'oping you might 'ave something to alleviate 'is suffering, so to speak.'

'Yes, it's difficult nursing loved ones, 'specially when you know they won't recover.' Mary nodded, a faraway look on her face, as she thought back to her grandmother and how painful it had been watching her waste away. She remembered how tired and weak she had felt as she tended to her every need, and how unpleasant some of it had been.

'Yes, Martha. I believe I can ease 'is pain.' The girls looked at each other, exchanging knowing glances, before Mary found a stool, reached up, and took small bottle from the shelf. She retrieved a few more bottles, ground some herbs, and added them to the liquid.

'That'll be tuppence, please.' Martha looked at Mary, a pensive frown forming on her face. She knew it should be more and was a bit affronted at the idea of her needing charity. 'It should really be thruppence ha'penny, but I know what it's like to nurse someone in their last moments.'

'Thanks Mary. You're a good'un. I won't forget this.' Martha's smile returned, now she could see it was just a simple act of kindness.

She had no idea what ingredients Mary had used but was as happy as she could be, knowing it would alleviate her father's suffering. Sure enough, the following morning she found him dead. She didn't cry. She was sick of crying; she had cried plenty throughout his illness: tears of exhaustion, tears of pain, tears of sorrow, and some tears that just seemed to fall for no reason. There had been days when she knew nothing but tears. So, today, instead of crying, she leant over and gently kissed his forehead.

'Goodbye,' she whispered, before kneeling to pray.

It wasn't that he left her with no money, but the little he had left her she would need. There was only her now and she'd be damned if she was going to end up working in the Jolly Sailor like so many other young orphan girls her age. Besides, she had a home and ways to earn her food but, nonetheless, funerals didn't come cheap and would cut deeply into the little money she had. So, she made the decision to bury her father on their land and if it meant digging his grave herself, then so be it. And that is exactly what she did. It took her a good few days, and her father was beginning to smell by the time she had finished. It wasn't as deep as she would've liked, but the need to get him out of the house strongly outweighed her capacity for more digging. She marked his grave with a small wooden cross made from some large twigs. It wasn't perfect, but he was buried, his grave marked, and she had prayed for his soul. John Wiggot had as much of a Christian burial as any man, and Martha had enough money to get her through the winter.

Over the next couple of years, Martha grew into a fine young woman; she had good morals and kept herself to herself. She made a fair living from the smallholding and her pickles and preserves were well-received at market. All gossip about her and her father had died with him, folks on the island weren't ones to speak ill of the dead. It was only the living who were the subject of local tittle- tattle.

Unlike the other girls on the island, well, all except Elsie Pearce, there were no local lads hanging around Martha Wiggot. Her body language made it perfectly clear she was not interested in a husband. Perhaps her father had taken more than a parental interest in her on occasion, or perhaps she just didn't want to nurse another sick man. Who knows? But whatever the reason,

Martha remained single and, at least for the time being, seemed happy to keep it that way. That was until the arrival of one Francis Derry.

---

1 ... Old Dorset slang for bewitched (also used to describe those cursed or enchanted)

Chapter 5
Saturday Sinners

When God calleth,
'Pon an 'oly man
Pious, sacred, an' true.
Watch 'e fall
by the way.
For no ministry
can abide,
When a wytch
abide there too.

Francis, or "Minister Derry" as he preferred, had been sent to the island following rumours that some of the islanders were not fully embracing the Methodist faith and were, in fact, still practicing "their old ways." Minister Derry was of the belief that anything being called "the old ways" was nothing other than wytchcraft, plain and simple.

So, Minister Derry was on a wytch hunt, but unlike the wytch hunters of old, he was expected to do it honourably and with legitimate evidence, and therein lay the problem. He knew, the same way that everyone knew Mary Flann was a wytch: local gossip, hushed whispers, hearsay, and an abundance of suspicious circumstances and events. The problem wasn't only that this didn't really amount to proper evidence. Mary was also popular, in the same way that her grandmother Irene had been popular. She ran the only apothecary on the island, could cure most common ailments, and ease the aches and pains of the elderly and overworked. This made it all very difficult to prove, and unfortunately for him, no less than John Wesley himself had put him in charge of doing just that. Somehow, he needed to find a way of proving that her, and a few others he suspected, were indeed practising wytchcraft.

Minister Derry brought with him his wife, a pleasant enough soul who, unlike her husband, wasn't given to superstition and had a kind word for everyone. She was also plagued with headaches and was a regular customer at Mary Flann's apothecary. Francis Derry made his feelings on the matter well-known to his wife, who, like all wives, completely disregarded his thoughts on the matter. For as long as Mary could ease her headaches, she was happy enough to deal with her, no matter what her husband said.

Under any other circumstances she may not have got off so lightly, but Minister Derry didn't have time to police his wife's activities; he was busily wytch hunting. And there was, of course, Martha Wiggot.

Mary, Bridie, and Elsie all regularly attended church, good Christians that they were. On a small island, appearances are everything. So, they always made sure to sit as near to the middle as possible; the back of the church was generally considered to be occupied by the least pious members of the community.

It was during Minister Derry's first sermon that he caught sight of Martha Wiggot; anybody with eyes could see he was infatuated with her from that moment.

Mary nudged Bridie and nodded towards the besotted minister who, for the last few minutes had appeared either unable or unwilling to avert his eyes from Martha. Bridie in turn nudged Elsie, and all three girls bit their lips or coughed to stifle their laughter as Minister Derry talked enthusiastically about the sanctity of marriage.

Tears rolled down the girls' faces as the words "thou shalt not commit adultery" tripped adulterously from his lips. For the rest of the service Mary, Bridie, and Elsie watched the eye contact between Francis Derry and Martha Wiggot.

'It's Mrs Derry I feel sorry for.' Elsie commented on the walk back to the apothecary.

'You're such an old romantic.' Bridie teased.

'Don't see 'ow that's a bad thing. I mean, if I was lucky enough to find an 'usband I'd be devastated if 'e went off with someone else.'

'It is a little naïve.' Mary interjected. 'Most of the men on this island, god-fearing or otherwise, 'ave found their way to the Jolly Sailor at least once. They are all Saturday sinners and Sunday repenters.'

'Well, my marriage would be different,' sighed Elsie. 'Just gotta find an 'usband first.'

'Any man would be damn lucky to 'ave you.' Bridie reassured.

'Except she don't want just any man, do ya, Elsie Pearce?' Mary nudged her and winked.

'Aw, don't tease 'er Mary. We could 'elp 'er ...'

'I've offered before, and she refused; didn't ya?'

Elsie sighed and shook her head.

'I just want 'im to notice me fair and square. That's all ... is that so much to ask?'

'No,' said Bridie, linking arms with Elsie 'It's 'ow it should be and 'e's a fool for not noticing.'

Elsie smiled weakly at Bridie. She knew her friends meant well, but they were both pretty girls. Mary could have had any boy she wanted, and Elsie just wanted one.

All Elsie had ever wanted was to be looked after, probably because that was all her mother wanted for her. A subject that, no matter how strong their marriage was, this was where her mother and father were in complete disagreement.

Elizabeth strongly believed her daughter should be married as soon as possible, for fear of her becoming an old maid. To this end, her mother spent a lot of time suggesting eligible young men for her daughter. Most of these were not young and were, more often than not, at least twice Elsie's age. Her father's stand on this came in the form of:

'For the love of God, leave the girl be. She's not much more than a child; she's plenty o' time to wed. Old maid my arse!'

Elsie, used to their bickering over her, tended to leave them to it but her mother's words cut deep, and she spent a lot of time dreaming about her perfect wedding.

It was a sad truth that Elsie wasn't the prettiest of the girls, but she was determined to find herself a husband, no matter what the cost. And in an ideal world—Elsie's ideal world, that man was Thomas Whistance.

Her clumsy approaches in that direction, however, went unnoticed. Elsie would smile if he passed by her, or she'd drop a handkerchief as he came out of the local alehouse. She'd practically tripped over him one time, as she left Mary Flann's apothecary, but none of it got her noticed.

Mary and Bridie had offered to help the only way they knew how, but Elsie wanted him to notice her the way she had noticed him.

Thomas Whistance wasn't an islander. He had come to the island in 1814 from Gloucester. He, like many other young men, local and Kimberlin, had come looking for work in the quarries. Quarrymen were in short supply as it was hard work and took an unwanted toll on those who worked there. Mary Flann healed many a quarry injury and would often shake her head in dismay at the savage brutality of their livelihood.

'This island is a crueller mistress than the ocean surrounding it could ever be.'

The afflicted would always attempt a weak nod or smile, grateful that someone recognised their plight. So far, Thomas had not needed Mary's services, but that too was only ever a matter of time.

Elsie believed different.

'You know my father is a quarryman an' 'e be the picture of 'ealth. You're just being dramatic, Mary Flann, like always.'

'Your father, Elsie Pearce, is a supervisor, always 'as been. An' the most dangerous thing 'e ever did was marry yer mother!'

Elsie looked at Bridie, who was trying her best to stifle a laugh. She glanced back at Mary who had likewise realised the humour in her outburst. And so, Elsie smiled too, shrugged her shoulders, and shook her head before adding:

''Appen you're right. 'Appen you're right.' At which point all three burst out laughing.

'Anyway,' Elsie commented, managing to catch her breath, and still smiling, 'I remain resolute.' She continued, 'We is the same age, and I believe it's a sign. I reckon we is made for each other. Cut from the same cloth if you will, 'e's another one born in the same year. I reckon 'tis fate—like it's written in the stars above ...' She mused dreamily, casting a wistful eye towards the sky.

'You do know that any one of us three could say that about 'im, don't you' Mary reminded her, but she didn't care.

'It's not the same an' you both well know it, because I loves 'im an' you don't.'

There was no arguing with that sort of logic, unless, of course, you happened to be Elsie's mother. She was fully aware of her daughter hopelessly mooning after Thomas Whistance and had tried to get her father to intervene at work on her behalf. But Joe Pearce was having none of it.

'You know, when I was your age Elsie Pearce, I had boys fallin' over themselves, I did. You clearly don't get your looks from me ... I despair of ever gettin' you wed. Perhaps you should have a word with that friend of yours ... What's her name again?' Elsie could feel the tears pricking her eyes. She very much doubted that any of that was true, but it hurt, nonetheless. Her mother could be a harsh woman at times and Elsie saw nothing to be gained by arguing over it.

'You know full well what 'er name is. It's Mary!'

'Yes, that's her, Mary; Mary Flann.'

With that, Elsie left the house sobbing all the way to Mary's cottage. She wasn't going there on account of her mother. She was there because she had already made up her mind to enlist Mary's help. She was simply tired of being unnoticed and unwanted. Likewise, she was sickened by her mother constantly trying to marry her off to unsuitable suitors.

It was time to take Mary up on her offer of help—because she wanted it—and not because her mother had suggested it.

Chapter 6
Skipping and Dropping

Twist the bindweed once for love.
Twist it twice for love that last.
Twist it hard, then, twist it fast,
And knot it best you can.
Starve till dewbit[1].
Skip till ye drop,
And say the name
of he who be hag rod[2].

'Quickly Mary, 'urry up.' Elsie urged. 'Please Mary, get that 'id away. I can 'ear Min'ster Derry's footsteps.'

''E don't realise 'ow distinct 'is footsteps is, that's for sure; a proper drawlatchet[3] that one is.' Bridie added, loosening the floorboard for Mary.

'Good job 'e is.' Elsie whined, having far more of a vested interest in this particular spell.

The last of the spell was safely concealed under a loose floorboard, just as Minister Derry rapped on the cottage door. 'Why, Mr Derry, what an 'onour to 'ave you call on our 'umble abode. What with you being a minister an' all.'

'Spare the platitudes, Mary Flann. I'm sure you are well aware why I'm here.' The girls looked at each other, shaking their heads, and feigning their best puzzled expressions.

'I know there is wytchcraft on this island, and I know you are guilty of such practices, Mary Flann.' He turned sharply and pointed to a rather skinny girl who was currently chopping vegetables.

'Dunno what you're talkin' about. We's just doin' our Christian duty: preparin' food for Granny Peters, ain't we girls?' The other two nodded, grateful to Mary Flann for taking the lead. Mary continued chopping vegetables, quite aware of the urgent need to finish her spell before it dried up and became impotent.

'Bridie's granny is proper poorly, as you well know Min'ister Derry, so we're just doin' our bit to 'elp an,' if you don't mind, we'd like to be getting' on with our chores, afore Bridie's granny takes a turn for the worse.'

'Or dies of starvation.' Bridie threw in just for good measure, causing Minister Derry to look back at the three of them. He knew they were practising wytchcraft, but the problem was that he couldn't prove it.

Once he had gone, Mary returned to her spell, finished it with a kiss, and handed it to Elsie Pearce.

'Now, don't forget Elsie. Keep it with you until you're wed. Oh, an' you need to starve till dewbit, an' afore you go abed you need to skip till you drop. Don't forget now, Elsie.'

'I won't, an' thanks Mary, you're a good friend; you both are.' She hugged both girls tightly, 'I won't forget this; I really won't.'

Elsie was out the door and headed for home before they had a chance to say goodbye.

Elsie followed her instructions methodically. Everyone knew that Mary's potions and the like worked and, while she had every faith in it, she was taking no chances either.

So, despite her mother's protests that a girl her age should eat afore bed, she politely retired to her bedchamber and skipped till she dropped.

Fortunately for Elsie, she lived in a large enough house with good rugs for her skipping and dropping not to be noticed. Although, if Mrs Pearce thought it would bring her youngest a husband, she would have skipped till she dropped herself.

As it was, Elsie followed Mary's instructions to the letter. She kept the small poppet in a tie-on pocket under her dress. It was her secret and only Mary and Bridie shared it.

✵

Then it happened. Elsie burst into the apothecary and made Bridie jump clear out of her skin. Mary, of course, was more composed.

'I'm going to assume 'e's noticed you,' Mary smiled. Bridie made enquiring gestures with her left hand, her right one clutching her heart, which was still racing from Elsie's entrance.

''E asked me if I'd go for a stroll with 'im after church on Sunday.' Her words seem to drift off into the ether, as Elsie, almost faint with excitement, recounted the whole story. She had passed him on the hill, as she was on her way to Chiswell. This time she had stumbled unintentionally, and it was none other than Thomas who had caught her.

'I tells you Mary, my 'eart 'as never beaten so fast ...'

'Mine 'as,' mumbled Bridie, just about regaining her breath.

'Shh, let 'er tell her story. Lord knows she's waited long enough.'

''E proper smiled at me, took my 'and, an' asked if I'd do 'im the 'onour of takin' a stroll with 'im this Sunday afternoon. *Me*? Do *'im* the 'onour? Can you believe it? I could scarcely get me words out; I must've sounded a proper idiot. Me mother'll never believe it.'

'Yes Elsie Pearce, I can believe it— can't we Bridie?' Bridie nodded.

'Course we can an' you just enjoy it, an' pay no 'eed to that mother of yours neither. And keep 'old of that poppet, don't let it go till yer wed.'

Within a year she was married to Thomas Whistance. It seemed he had noticed her all along and just needed a bit of a nudge in the right direction, so to speak.

Thomas and Elsie were a lovely couple, and it was good to see her happy. Even her mother was nicer to her now she was no longer her and her father's responsibility. To be honest, brutally honest, she'd have been happy if Elsie had married the local drunk.

The poppet stayed with her until the morning after her wedding day. She awoke early, while Thomas slept, and walked down to the beach. Taking the little poppet out from her pocket, she gazed upon it, just for a moment. Then she thanked it for bringing her Thomas, kissed it, as she had seen Mary do so often, and cast it into the ocean.

'May our love be ever as wide and deep as the mighty ocean.' With that, she, Elsie Whistance, nee Pearce, turned and walked back up the hill to her beloved Thomas.

Later that year, Thomas returned to Gloucester with his new bride, having secured a good position as a groundsman with a tied cottage. Elsie wondered if Mary had been in some way responsible.

Her way, perhaps, of ensuring the quarry didn't claim him. Whatever the truth, that was the last time either Mary or Bridie saw Elsie.

---

1 ... Old Dorset slang for a bite to eat before breakfast
2 ... Old Dorset slang for bewitched
3 ... Old Dorset slang for a person who walks slowly and lazily

Chapter 7
His Beloved Martha

When a wytch be,
A watchin' ye,
Then turn yer face aside.
For should ye,
Let her see
into thine eyes.
Then, yer soul she'll take
An' more besides.

Minister Derry was no fool, and he suspected that Elsie's sudden good fortune was the work of Mary Flann. It ate away at him. More than anything, he wanted to be free to be with his beloved Martha. However, he was a devout man of God, and so, his faith, prevented him from taking the same course of action. Sometimes his God was as much a curse, as he was a blessing. Mary Flann, likewise, was far from dim. She kept a cautious eye on the minister's comings and goings.

Francis Derry was not the happiest of men, but he liked to believe he was one of the most devout. His wife may have believed him, or turned a blind eye, perhaps even loved him. Mary Flann, however, being emotionally unattached to him, remained ever cautious.

Mary saw him making the journey to and from Martha Wiggot's and kept a close eye and mental note of how often he visited and how long he was there. She fully understood why a man like Francis Derry would be interested in Martha Wiggot. What she didn't understand was what Martha saw in him; judging by the looks that passed between them in church, she was as besotted by him as he was by her. Not one for getting in the way of true love, Mary would keep her distance and cause him no angst for as long as he left her in peace. But, like most things, it was always only ever a matter of time.

Chapter 8
Wytchcraft

Hell, itself knows no scorn,
No fury, curse, or spell.
No blessing from God
Can dry the tears,
Nor quell the screams,
Of a mother
Whose child's stillborn.

'Come quick Mary, it's Annie Stone. She's strugglin' real bad—quick Mare.'

Mary grabbed her midwifery bag and followed Bridie out into the cold February night. The wind coming off the sea bit hard and she held her shawl tightly, clinging onto it for dear life.

It was too cold for conversation and, on nights such as these, Mary felt her talents were a curse, as much as they were a blessing.

She didn't really need to ask Bridie what was wrong; she assumed Annie had gone into labour and was struggling with the delivery. Annie was a slight woman and hardly the build for childbearing. Mary could hear her screams of pain a good couple of hundred yards away.

She quickened her pace and made it just in time for the next scream.

'Come, come, Annie. We're 'ere now—Bridie fetch me some 'ot water an' cloths. Let's bring this babe into the world.'

Bridie and Mary had brought enough babies into the world to know that this was not going to be easy. But they were also experienced enough to know that reassuring the mother was always the priority. In the dim candlelight they could see the baby had the cord around its neck and, worse than that, it was torn. Mary looked at Bridie—both girls could see the baby had been dead a good few hours. There was nothing either of them could do, other than remove the baby and save Annie any further discomfort.

Mary had brought herbs and tinctures to relieve the pain. Annie, still unaware of the baby's death, was grateful for anything that eased her pain. The two girls worked as best they could, but Annie's screams of pain were nothing compared to the cries of anguish she let out upon realising the baby she had carried for nine months was not to be. Bridie and Mary had to prise the infant from her mother's arms. Mary prepared something to help the mother sleep, but Annie still sobbed, even then.

Understandably, Annie was never the same emotionally. The trauma of it weighed heavy and, despite Mary's tinctures and remedies, such was Annie's melancholy that all it took was one well meaning visit from Bridie's grandmother, Lily.

One hour later and Lily had convinced Annie that Mary was responsible for the ill that had befallen her. All the good that Mary Flann had done in the community: all those mothers and babies she had saved, the ails she had cured, and the comfort she had offered to those leaving this world—all that was gone the day Annie Stone told Minister Derry that she believed Mary Flann practised wytchcraft. Even then, damming accusations don't amount to proper evidence when they come from a grieving mother and a bitter old woman. He, Minister Derry, still needed, to have something more tangible to present to John Wesley. Nobody wanted to make the same mistakes as had been made a few centuries earlier.

Chapter 9
Wednesday Afternoons

'E who falls by the way
From a righteous path.
Will surely,
Reap what 'e 'as sown.
Not through the
Thunderous rage, of
His beloved God.
But by incurring,
The wytch's wrath.

Mary, in order to keep up appearances, still went to church with Bridie every Sunday, regular as clockwork. This made Minister Derry's one-woman wytch hunt very difficult. The finger pointing and gossip was only ever about Mary—never Bridie. Bridie's family were involved in politics and Bridie's father had even sat as a Justice of the Peace for a while. There are some families you are better off not messing with, and Bridie's was one of those families.

''Is sermons is almost as passionate as 'is Wednesday afternoons with a certain Miss Wiggot.' Mary giggled, nudging Bridie. 'I mean, you'd think 'e'd smile more, all things considered.'

''Appen misery is a side effect of ministry.' Bridie mused back, during what was proving to be a particularly gruelling church service. The words "vile and wretched sinners" seemed to come up a lot and always with a glance in their direction.

''E's certainly miserable, I'll give you that,' agreed Mary, 'but 'e do 'ave a weakness, an if 'e looks over 'ere one more time ...'

'Ooh, you wouldn't Mary.'

'Why not? 'E almost disrupted Elsie's chance at 'appiness, an' 'e listened to Annie Stone's ramblin's ... an' yer granny's. B'sides, 'e ain't 'appy, you said so yerself.'

'But Elsie's 'appily married, an' Annie's quieted down now an' my granny can't 'ave too much longer left, so there's no 'arm done is there? I say we just leave 'im to 'is misery.'

''E's out to get us—you know 'e is Bridie'

'Well, 'e's gotta prove it, ain't 'e?'

'Right, well the church is not the only object of 'is affections is it now? Y' know 'e be sweet on Martha Wiggot … I sees 'im on a Wens'day. I tells yer Bridie,'e do limp in an' swagger out— an' I reckon I knows just 'ow to get 'im.'

Once Mary Flann got a notion in her head there was no stopping her. It was obvious that the indiscretions of Francis Derry weren't going to last much longer.

Chapter 10
Sleep Baby Sleep

Take the caul of a stillborn child,
Wrap it in the woolle
of a black sheep.
Mix with juice of belladonna,
An' nail it in a wooden box,.
An' bury it neath the porch.
An, baby will forever sleep.
A sprinkling of my monthly blood,
An' my wytchery silent keep.

Mary Flann and Bridie Peters cavorted wildly around the small wooden box, which was positioned in the middle of the cottage's kitchen floor, chanting all the while.

'Sleep baby sleep, sleep baby sleep'

Bridie may not have approved, but she wasn't about to leave Mary to do it by herself; besides he wasn't out to get *them*. Just Mary!

They danced until they collapsed through sheer exhaustion and later, in the pale moonlight, they made the trip to Martha Wiggot's cottage on the east side of the island. This was the designated burial plot.

'Yer know this ain't right, Mare? She ain't never done nothin' to us, an' punishin' 'im by 'urtin' 'er just don't seem proper.'

'Got any better ideas then?'

Bridie went quiet.

'Nah, thought not ... now shh.' Mary held her finger to her lips, just to be sure Bridie got the message. She did. They continued in silence. When they reached Martha's house, both girls, as quiet as mice, dug a hole just deep enough next to Martha's doorstep. Mary Flann kissed the box before placing it in the ground and covering it over. She kissed all her spells, whether curse or cure. She said it put something of her in it, so the spirits knew who was asking for their help. She then patted the cool earth, adding a final

'Sleep, baby sleep'

Sure enough, within days Martha Wiggot began to cough, and by the time a week had passed it was obvious that she was sick. She was pale, and over the coming weeks she grew thinner and weaker. Minister

Derry had said it was his Christian duty to provide proper medical care, which, of course, didn't involve either the apothecary or Mary Flann. Instead, he called in a doctor from the county town—but within three months Martha Wiggot was dead.

'If 'e'd asked, I'd 've saved 'er; yer knows I would, but 'e didn't.' Mary offered, as her and Bridie watched Minister Derry bury the love of his life early in the spring of 1815. Both girls knew that it was Mary's spell that had caused it.

Bridie felt dreadful and, despite their long friendship, wished she'd had no part in it, but she did. When all was said and done, she was, after all, a Flann; Mary reasoned that a broken Minister would have no interest in a wytch hunt.

To some extent, this was true; he wasn't none too interested in anything after Martha's death, not even his faith— and least of all wytches.

Chapter 11
A Man of God

In the darkest night of them all
Heed the wytch's call
Lose control an' feel the pain
That's hidden in this verse
Feel the guilt of all your sins
For such is the wytch's curse.

Minister Derry and his wife had been entertaining guests and it had been a long day. While he may have been willing to sit up half the night discussing the Bible with fellow ministers, his wife was not. She had made her excuses a few hours and several bottles of wine earlier.

When he finally headed for bed, he noticed how dark the night was and how much darker his life had become without Martha Wiggot. He would give up everything to have her back. He could hear his wife faintly snoring through the cottage wall and thought how his beloved Martha was so much more attractive than his she-goat of a wife.

He lay there in bed, trying hard not to think about it; after all, such thoughts led to stirrings, and he could already feel the movement beneath his nightshirt. Two minutes of thinking about Martha Wiggot and he was aroused. He, being a man of God, considered satiating one's lust with no chance of a child to be abhorrent. His lust was his curse and the more he tried not to think of her, the more aroused he became. Eventually it became too much to bear and, in a trance like state, unaware of anything except Martha, and with tears rolling down his cheeks, he stumbled his way to his wife's chamber. She was asleep, yet without either thought or care for the woman he had married, he threw the covers aside, grabbed her legs, and dragged her to the foot of the bed.

She awoke, afraid and shaken. She screamed at him, protesting the intrusion and the violation of her privacy, but to no avail. He placed his hand firmly over her mouth and spared precious little time reminding her that she was his wife and, as such, should fulfil her wifely duty. Within minutes he had aggressively removed her bloomers, hitched up his nightshirt, and thrust his cock into her. Such was his lust that all reason and compassion fell to the wayside. His desire was animalistic, brutal, and obsessive. The pious minister was oblivious to either his god, or his wife, who sobbed constantly throughout what was a mercifully quick event, but one that would doubtless leave her scarred. As soon as he was done, he released his grip on her thighs, and exited both her and her chamber in silence.

The following morning, he was awoken a little later than usual by his wife bringing him his breakfast tray. He could see the fear and hatred in her eyes and was promptly reminded of the previous night. She put the tray down by the bed as normal and went to leave, but before she could he grabbed her wrist.

'I'm sorry. I'm so very sorry. Please look at me.' She turned to face him. 'I'm so very, very sorry. You deserve far better than the miserable wretch I have become, and I will endeavour to be just that. Better. A better man, a better husband—in every way better. If I have to spend the rest of my days making it up to you, then I will do so gladly.' She nodded. He let her go and as she walked away, he noticed that she was walking with some discomfort. He despised who he had become, and he knew it would be a long time before she felt safe around him, if ever.

The following night things seemed more normal. He was only moments behind his wife as he headed to bed and, passing her chamber, he heard her key twist in the lock. His heart was heavy. He had lost Martha and abused his wife, so that even she, who had promised in God's eyes to love, honour, and obey him, loathed the very sight of him. With all the sorrow one man could bear, he put on his nightshirt and got into bed. His thoughts that night were far from erotic and arousal was a distant, less than pleasant, memory.

He was finally drifting off to sleep when he heard the sound of faint scratching. Assuming it to be mice or, worse still, rats in the pantry, he rolled over and tried to ignore it. It continued with no let-up, until he was forced to get up and investigate. He grabbed the candle he kept beside the bed and, shielding the flame from draughts, headed for the pantry. A thorough inspection found no evidence of either mice or rats and so, none the wiser, he returned to bed.

Once again, the scratching began and this time he listened more intently. It was faint and he believed it couldn't be anything other than a small rodent somewhere in the house. Exhausted, and unwilling to search the entire house, he gave up and fell asleep.

The scratching continued, but this time it filled his dreams. He was with Martha at her house; she was beautiful, yet otherworldly, resembling the faerie folk of the Irish. She was waif-like, and she sang and danced around him with her arms outstretched, sensuous, captivating, and as beautiful as ever. Yet, throughout it all, she remained tantalisingly out of reach and her song was too faint to make out the words. Gradually she faded into the distance and her singing was once again replaced by the scratching. As the image of her faded, so the scratching grew louder and louder, until eventually there was darkness and all he could hear was the scratching. It was almost deafening. And then it stopped—just like that—as suddenly as it had started. It stopped and there was silence.

Then, without warning, the image of Martha beneath the ground and scratching inside the coffin caused him to abruptly awaken. He wanted to scream, but he was paralysed, unable to either move or speak. Eventually, he exhaled and, shaking with fear, his mind rapidly re-traced his dream. By nature, Minister Derry was neither suspicious, auspicious, or superstitious, but could his beautiful Martha have been buried alive?

There was only one way to find out.

Chapter 12
Digging a Grave

That which a wytch 'as caused,
An' God hath lay to rest,
Should ne'er be disturbed,
Lest it be cursed instead o' blest.
For you be at the crossroads
Betwixt madness,
and mortal death,
An' the curse be 'pon you'
Til your final breath.

There were procedures for exhuming a body; even in 1815, there needed to be a good reason for digging up that which God had laid to rest.

While there was plenty of gossip, hearsay, and tittle-tattle concerning the relationship between Minister Derry and Martha Wiggot, there had been nothing that could be construed as actual proof.

However, the actions that followed his dream that night were blasphemous and verging on insanity.

With no proper permission, or any authority beyond his own, Minister Derry practically ran to the churchyard. Once there, he found Old Fossor digging a grave for a fellow due for burial that afternoon.

He practically dragged Old Fossor to Martha's grave, demanding that he dig her up, there and then.

'But Min'ster Derry, I can't be diggin''er up wiv'out p'missions—t'ain't right.'

'Just do it man.'

Old Fossor hesitated and, before he could get another word out, Minister Derry grabbed the shovel and began digging. A crowd gathered, and inevitably the sobbing and inconsolable Minister was taken to one side by the local doctor.

It took several hours, but eventually a calmer Minister Derry was taken to his house. The matter, for the time being, like Martha, was laid to rest.

However, following the near exhumation of Martha Wiggot, people grew concerned as to just how pious the good Minister Derry might be. After all, I mean, who digs up a soul that's been laid to rest, based on no more than a bad dream?

But still the dreams continued.

Chapter 13
Just out of Reach

Your dreams will
Lead you to drinky[1,]
You will shake an' quob[2.]
When mornin's piece proud,
wiv only yerself around
Where be yer god then?
Where be he to?
Nowhere!
T'is just your sorrow an' you.

Minister Derry's wife had become pregnant shortly after Martha Wiggot's death and he, Minister Derry, had done all he could to ease her confinement. Everything that is, except love her. That space was solely reserved for his beloved Martha.

His wife's pregnancy had, however, taken the gossip away from his "breakdown" in the churchyard. The local gossip was now focused on "poor Mrs Derry" and how sad it was that she was carrying his child while he obviously loved another.

Minister Derry's dreams continued, beginning every night with the same scratching.

Over time they progressed. The first night following the attempted exhumation, the scratching was followed by the window rattling. He reasoned this could well be the wind, although on the following night, he thought he saw a glimpse of Martha outside the window.

The dreams became more and more vivid as the days drifted by, turning slowly to weeks, and before long a month had passed. Eventually, the scratching was followed by Martha coming in through the window. Later, not only was she coming in, but she was dancing and singing. More importantly, she was always just out of reach.

Sometimes the scratching was louder. Sometimes the singing was louder, and he could make out the odd word or two. He recognised the tune as something Martha used to sing a lot, but he couldn't remember the words. Sometimes Martha was closer in his dreams, other times she was further away.

Most mornings he could feel the bulge beneath his nightshirt. Some mornings he remembered Martha's touch, her breasts, and the way she felt, and he would have to alleviate his lust regardless of scripture. Other mornings he would remember his vows to God. Always he remembered the promise he had made to his wife.

Despite the scratching, his dreams were the closest he could get to his beloved Martha Wiggot, and he had initially taken to drinking more in order to sleep earlier. This later became replaced by laudanum which, of course, was purchased from Mary's apothecary by his wife.

'See Bridie, we've got 'im. 'E ain't so int'rested in us now, is 'e?' Mary gloated, as she packaged the laudanum ready for his wife to collect.

'No, 'appen 'e ain't Mare.' Bridie knew Mary was right, but she still believed it wasn't right that Martha had died because of them. Their actions may have been a means to an end, but surely there could have been another, better way.

✪

It was several months after Martha Wiggot's death, and a good few weeks into his laudanum use, when Minister Derry finally remembered the song.

Perhaps it was the laudanum, which made him sleep deeper, or perhaps it was his own memory. Perhaps, he had even heard the other girls around the island singing it. Who knows?

But remember it he did.

---

1 ... Old Dorset slang for drunk
2 ... Old Dorset slang for shiver

77

Chapter 14
The Scent of Belladonna

Plant a tree by the front step,
While ye is young an' peart.
Plant a tree, so it do grow
An' wiv it our love will grow,
An' our chil'ren won't get hurt.

Martha Wiggot's house had stood empty for a year after her death; Minister Derry had continued to pay the rent on it. Everyone knew this and it had been a taboo subject in the Derry household, in the same way that any discussion about Minister Derry spending his evenings there was also forbidden. As a result of his remembering the song, he headed up to Martha's home one sunny afternoon to plant a tree.

He plunged the shovel into the soft earth and heard a gentle thud as it hit the small wooden coffin that Mary Flann and Bridie Peters had buried there.

He fell to his knees and continued digging the earth away with his hands, quickly revealing the coffin.

He prised the lid open to reveal its contents: the dried remains of a caul, some black wool, and there was no mistaking the scent of belladonna; and all of it had been nailed in a small coffin. He knew this was wytchcraft, and he knew exactly where to look. Mary Flann.

There was never a man with greater purpose than Minister Derry that afternoon. He marched straight down to Mary Flann's cottage and flung open her front door without knocking and without warning. He slammed the coffin down on the table in front of her.

'You will pay for this, Mary Flann—you and all those like you on this island. God's house is not a place for the likes of you. You wait—you will pay.'

With that, Mary went straight round to find Bridie Peters, and related the whole event, followed by, '... an' 'e'll get 'is too.'

'Oh, Mary, 'aven't we done enough damage? You know what could 'appen to the likes of us don't you?'

Mary looked thoughtful.

'But we can't let 'im get away with this. Surely you don't want 'im to win. Does ya?'

'No, but I at least need to know what 'e's planning before I make a move or a decision. We can't decide whether we let 'im win or lose if we dunna know what the game is, can we?'

'No, I suppose not.'

Mary was pacified for the moment.

Chapter 15

Insanity

Feel thy loss caused by my wrath,
As you lose all control.
You're torrididdle[1],
An' all but broken,
Now beat me if you dare.
Oh, heed the wrack
of all you've done,
And know
I'm always there.

Minister Derry's wife took her place at the front of the church with young Master Derry still only a babe in arms. It was the first time Mrs Derry had been seen in church since she announced her pregnancy.

Time passes quickly and, for most islanders, Martha Wiggot was fast becoming little more than a distant memory. That was not the case for Minister Derry, his wife, Mary Flann, and Bridie Peters. Martha was still fresh in all their memories. But today was Easter Sunday and, as such, was all about resurrection and rebirth.

It was a warm sunny morning when Mary Flann and Bridie Peters headed to church. Both of them were still reeling after Minister Derry's warning to Mary a few days earlier. They were sure others could sense their apprehension as they entered the church and took their seats towards the back.

The church was well attended that morning, with many a Sunday repenter present. There was even a couple of other ministers in the congregation.

No sooner had the doors closed, than Minister Derry began to speak. It was one of those speeches that those present would never forget. It would seem it wasn't just Mary Flann he'd burst in on that day.

'It has come to my attention that several of you have continued practising your ungodly rituals.'

He began reeling off several names. Of course, Mary was at the top of the list, but it seemed that once he started, he was unable to stop. The list of people accused continued until every member of the congregation had been named—all fifty of them, including

Preacher Whittle and Minister Hinde.

'Every last one of you can get out. Not one of you is welcome in this church ever again. EVER. Do you hear me? Now GET OUT!'

This was insanity.

The only ones left inside the church were his wife and son, and she probably wanted to leave more than anyone.

There they were, fifty of them, standing outside the church, each looking to the other trying to comprehend exactly what had just happened. Eventually Bridie Peters spoke.

She may have been in cahoots with Mary Flann, and on the surface may have seemed nothing special to casual passers-by, but her family had money and when money talks, everyone listens.

'Why don't we use my grandfather's old store as a place of worship. Just for now. It's clean an' warm. An' we 'ave two preachers who can take turns in min'stering. What d'you say?'

Surprisingly, they all agreed. Even Preacher Whittle and Minister

83

Hinde were agreeable. They may have both been Methodist ministers, but they were two very different people and their approach to Ministering was just as different. But both were happy with the suggestion that they could alternate their services.

It seemed things were settled until Mrs Hinde pointed out that a church does need a name.

'All churches have names. It won't seem right if it don't have a name.'

'I know,' piped up Mary Flann, "e's just accused all of us of wytchcraft. All of us.' She reiterated. 'So, why don't we call it Conj'rer's Lodge?'

Bridie's heart sank, and she looked from face to face. Mary was shameless all right, but even for her, this seemed a step too far.

Mary smiled at Bridie, whose face was a picture as far as Mary was concerned.

''Ave a little faith.' She whispered, nudging Bridie gently. Bridie glared at her. 'No. Look, Bridie ... look.' Mary urged, nodding towards the rest of the congregation. Bridie rolled her eyes, as she realised the rest of the congregation gathered outside the church were, in fact, considering Mary's idea.

'I think it's a good idea and it would make him look like the fool that he is. Let's face it, he hasn't been right since Martha Wiggot died.' Preacher Whittle's wife chirped.

There was a lot of murmuring and nodding.

Mary nudged Bridie, directing her gaze to the root she was twisting behind her back. Bridie couldn't help but smile at her cousin. She was. without a doubt, a Flann woman through and through.

So, on that warm Easter Sunday morning in 1816, Conjurer's Lodge was born.

---

1 ... Old Dorset slang for bewildered, verging on madness

Chapter 16
A Dark Winter Moon

For every curse
P'rhap's there's a cure.
An' for every cruelty,
Something is born
That be gentle and pure.
An' the world turns the wheel
Of time once more,
An' leads you to
the wytch's door.

As with all things, time heals all wounds and despite the bitter feelings between the congregations of the church and the Lodge, time did eventually heal the rift. Derry had been replaced by Minister Dunbar, who in 1826 attended a meeting in Bristol to discuss a reconciliation. However, there are occasions when even time and God need a helping hand, and this came in the form of Mrs Brackenbury. It was she who took the initiative to heal the divided community. Slowly and surely the Lodge members found their way back to the Methodist Church.

Conjurer's Lodge itself would remain forever woven into the island's rich tapestry, although the events leading up to its creation would be lost amid the hushed whispers of those trying to find a way to live as a community once more.

Mary and Bridie continued their "practices" but even they were much quieter about it. Few noticed two young women, disappearing into the shadows on a warm summer's evening, or braving the elements to conjure the spirits of Chesil Beach under a dark winter moon.

Mary's apothecary had suffered little financial damage despite the accusations levied against her. It would seem the potency of her tinctures and potions were far greater than her reputation as a wytch.

Portland may have been a small island, but it had a long memory, and the Flann women's bloodline was as much a part of it as the ocean that surrounded it.

Minister Derry had moved away shortly after his wife became ill. "Poor Mrs Derry" as she had become known had been taken ill with consumption.

There were many whispers as to her affliction being caused by the supernatural. Sometimes, the finger was even pointed at the ghost of Martha Wiggot. After all, hadn't her husband disturbed Martha's final resting place. Sometimes it was said that this was his punishment, sent by God. Precious few were brave enough to accuse Mary Flann of having a part in it.

Bridie Peters had married John Pearce, in one of several weddings that took place in the Conjurer's Lodge and had given birth to a baby boy the following year, Jack.

Mary too had a child, a daughter, Rosie Flann, who like her was born without a father or certainly not one she'd ever know the name of. Both children were five years old when the Lodge closed its doors for good.

It was a few years since Francis Derry had been replaced by Minister Dunbar. And it was Minister Dunbar, who, in 1826 attended the meeting in Bristol to discuss a reconciliation.

But it was Mrs Brackenbury who finally got things moving.

It was a beautiful summers day when Old Mrs Brackenbury, preacher Robert's widow practically marched past the apothecary with Squire Roberts, an old friend of her husband.

'Ha! Now she'll take no nonsense off the menfolk. 'Appen she maybe old, but that Mrs Brackenbury—well now, she's a force to be reckoned with. I tell you Bridie if anyone can sort it, it's 'er.'

'Yep 'appen you're right there. She scares me that's fer sure. So, them men-folks won't know what's 'it 'em.'

They both giggled, at the thought but sure enough two days later the Lodge closed its doors. The following Sunday the former congregation of Conjurer's Lodge was welcomed back to the Methodist Church.

Minister Dunbar's sermon was all about healing the rift between the parishioners. He hoped that this would see an end to the years of anxiety and struggle, with the words "turning the other cheek" cropping up here and there.

Bridie and Mary no longer sat together as Bridie now attended church with her husband and child. Mary, likewise, attended with Rosie, but both women smiled as they remembered giggling during Minister Derry's sermons as he stared cow-eyed at Martha Wiggot.

News eventually reached the island of Mrs Derry's death, several years after they had moved away.

"appen she died of a broken 'eart—wouldn't you? Well, I mean it ain't like 'e loved 'er or anythin'" Mary mused as she prepared a tincture for Bridie's husband who had recently developed a chesty cough.

'D'you really believe that Mare?'

"appen I do Bridie, 'appen I do. You seen 'im that day, 'e, lost all sensibility. I mean, 'e weren't smart at the best of times, but slingin' 'is 'ole congregation out—actions of a madman. If anything, it's 'is son I feel sorry for ... Derry got all 'e deserved. But then, I told you 'e would'

Bridie just nodded; Martha's death had never sat right with her.

"appen you did Mare—'appen you did'

✡

The rain outside was torrential and Mary, and Bridie were busy in the Apothecary. There had been a delivery of some of the more unusual herbs and roots, and Mary was keen to try them out.

Jack and Rosie were sat in the corner playing with one of Mary's unused poppets, which to Rosie was a fine rag doll.

'Ma Jack's bein' 'orrible.'

'Shh, just play nice' Mary snapped, but the squabble continued, getting gradually more heated, and eventually resulting in Jack pulling Rosie's hair.

Rosie let out a loud screech and screwed up her face in anger.

Mary marched straight over to the bickering children, cuffed them both around the back of the head, and swiftly removed the root from Rosie's tiny fingers.

Printed in the UK
by
clocbookprint.co.uk